ESAPHER AND THE WIZARD

By Lucille Jon

Esapher was a beautiful maiden who lived with her

aunt, who was said to have strange powers. Esapher did

not believe the tales that had been told concerning her

Aunty because she loved her very much. Her Aunty was the only parent that she had because her parents died when she was a very little girl.

She had heard tales that her Aunty, whose name was Salo, had been the one who had killed her parents with witchcraft. Esapher had noticed that there was a certain room in the house that she was not allowed to enter. Her Aunt Salo kept the key to the room around her neck and Esapher had no way of opening the door because the lock on the door was especially made to be opened by the key that her Aunt Salo wore around her neck.

Most of the young ladies Esapher's age were given in marriage. Esapher was pretty well lonely, for her school companions were now mothers and housewives. Her aunty had told Esapher that there was a lad in the North Country that she would meet someday and marry.

"But how do you know it, Aunt Salo?" Esapher would ask.

"It is a prediction, my child."

Therefore Esapher had settled down to being an old maid, trying to wait patiently for the lad from the North Country to come and take her hand in marriage. But the lad never came. By the time Esapher was twenty-one, the lad never showed up, twenty-two, twenty-three, he had never come. She was beginning to get impatient.

"I shall not wait for the lad," she told her Aunty. "I am going out in search of a husband, for I shall be too old soon."

"Please do not leave me, Esapher," her Aunty begged. "You are all I have. Surely the lad will come soon."

Esapher decided to stay longer with her Aunty because she did hate to leave her. By the time she was thirty the young man had not come. Therefore Esapher bade her Aunty goodbye and left.

This made her Aunty very angry. She was really a witch and she unlocked the forbidden room. She entered it. She had all kinds of weird devices in the room. She had a pen with some squabs in it. She lifted one of the squabs from the pen. After picking three feathers, she said, "Esapher must suffer three years for departing from me, one feather for each ten years that I have kept her." She threw the feathers into a pot of brew, lit the fire and boiled the brew. As she did so, her face took on the form of a witch. She became rather a haunting-looking sight. Her hair became witchy long and her fingernails grew long also. Had Esapher seen her Aunty now she would not have believed it.

Esapher had taken the path through the woods to Halmiton. She had harnessed her horse Sweep, that her Aunty had given her for her birthday. Therefore she had a way of transportation. She did not take many clothes with her. Beyond Halmiton was a fork in the road pointing in three directions.

"Which road shall I take, Sweep?" Esapher asked her horse.

The horse Sweep nodded his head to the side road on the left that led to an unknown direction, because the road sign had been up so long that the letters had faded.

"Well, Sweep, I shall take that road, then. I do not know where we are going, but we are on our way."

About five miles down the road they came to a spring. Esapher was hungry. So she took from her bag a few sandwiches and sat upon the ground under a shady tree to eat. Esapher told Sweet to eat the green grass and that she would give him some sugar that she had.

"I will always take good care of you, Sweep," Esapher told him, "because somehow I feel that you are all I have now."

After they had eaten and rested, Esapher climbed upon Sweep and off they started again. They were coming into the suburbs of another town. There, at the edge of the woods, was a little cottage. Esapher decided to stop there and see if she could rest and perhaps refresh herself and get a night's lodging. It was especially fine for Sweep, because he could graze there in the morning before they started off again.

She knocked upon the door but she did not receive any answer. She knocked twice, then thrice, but she received no answer. She pushed the door open and in she walked. The little house was nicely furnished in the living room, dining room, bedroom, and kitchen, yet it looked as though only a bachelor lived there. There were no lady's clothes there in the closet, and there were no curtains at the windows. I wonder who lives here, Esapher thought. Well, since there is definitely no one here, I must make myself at home until they return.

She found feed in the back of the house for Sweep and a large pot in which she poured water for Sweep. He was very very thirsty. After Esapher had eaten some of the food that she found there, biscuits in the cupboard and

rhubarb jelly, she sat down to relax, wondering when

someone would return.

She remembered seeing a jug of wine in the

cupboard. She poured herself a glass of wine. After

drinking it, she fell into a doze. She was so tired that she

fell across the bed and went to sleep.

The next day when she awoke she was surprised to

find out that the owner of the house had not returned.

Esapher dressed herself and went out to feed Sweep.

She gave him some of the oats that she found there in the

back. There was plenty of firewood cut and stacked near

the house, so Esapher started a fire and cooked herself a nice breakfast.

All day she waited for the owner to return. But no one came. Esapher did not have any particular destination in mind, so she stayed on. For two weeks she waited for the owner to come, but no one came. The little house was so nice that Esapher decided to stay there until someone claimed it.

She harnessed Sweep and off they drove into town to buy material to make curtains for the little house. She also had to buy food, because the supply of food there at the little house was almost gone. Two months went by and

Esapher had become very fond of her home.

One day she was singing and setting the table after

fixing a lovely meal. She had just sat down to eat when

she heard a knock on the door after someone, having tried

to open it, had found it locked.

"Well, this is it," thought Esapher. "The owner must

be coming."

In walked a dusty fellow who looked as if he had been

traveling many a day. He stopped short and looked

Esapher up and down when he saw her.

"Well, my," he said. "What a beautiful surprise!"

"I am sorry," Esapher said. "I have been waiting for your return. This is your house, isn't it?"

"Yes, it is," the fellow told Esapher.

"I am just having dinner," Esapher told him. "Won't you have some? I know you must be hungry and tired."

"Quite so," answered the fellow. "My name is Zoak. What is ours? Don't tell me," he said "I know. It is Esapher."

"That's right," Esapher said, "but how did you know?"

"I have a way of knowing things, my dear."

After Zoak had washed the dirt and grime from his hands and face he became a rather handsome gentleman. He sat down opposite Esapher to eat the delicious food that she had prepared.

"I say, my dear girl, did you know I would return today?" he asked Esapher.

"No. I had no way of knowing," Esapher answered. "Why do you ask?"

"You had prepared a double supply of vittles,"

"I always do," Esapher told the gentleman. "I always do. I pretend that I am eating with my husband."

"Your husband! But where is he?" asked Zoak.

"Oh," said Esapher laughingly. "I did not mean that I have a husband really. I was pretending to have one."

"Ah, and that makes it nicer," said Zoak. "Because eating with a beautiful maiden is a rare thing for me. This I have not had time to engage in. I have been kept so busy. My job, that is," said Zoak.

"How old are you?" Esapher asked Zoak.

"Personal, my dear, very personal," answered Zoak. "But, of course, if you want to know, I am at the point of thirty-nine."

"Have you never married?" asked Esapher.

"No, never," answered Zoak. "I have no time for the like. But with a maiden like you around I could jolly well settle down."

"You speak such pleasant things to me," Esapher told Zoak.

After they had finished eating, Esapher went into the kitchen to wash dishes.

"Hold now, my dear, I will help you clear the rubbish from the dishes."

"Oh, that's all right," Esapher told him. "I do not mind. You perhaps are still tired, so why don't you relax."

"Quite so, quite so, I say. You do have a brilliant mind."

Zoak sat down in his rocker and smoked. After Esapher had finished the dishes, she told Zoak that she had to be on her way and it was nice meeting him, and she would hate to depart from the little house.

"But, my dear, it is nearly dark. You may get lost, so stay on. I will not harm you. You can be my housekeeper if you'd rather. There is no talk concerning that and after all there is no one to gossip. Our neighbors are so far

away.”

That Esapher knew, for it had taken her and Sweep a

day and a night to go into town. Esapher had fallen in love

with Zoak and she did not want to leave anyway. She

thought that if she stayed on as his housekeeper he might

decide to keep her on as his wife. As he sat in his rocker

with his head thrown back, how she wanted to kiss him.

“Does your pipe give you a thrill?” Esapher asked

Zoak.

"Well now I suppose so," answered Zoak. "Want to try it?"

"I never have smoked one," Esapher said. "Yes, please, perhaps a little draw won't hurt."

So Esapher took a puff from the pipe.

"Oh!" said Esapher. "What a nauseating experience. How can you stand it?"

"Well, my dear, I am used to it."

Esapher was very near Zoak now, so she bent to kiss him and kissed him full on the lips.

"Now," he asked. "Why did you break into my laughter with a kiss? I declare you are more thrilling than the pipe, but you need a spanking and to be put to bed."

Esapher felt strange. She had no intention of kissing him in the middle of his laughter concerning her and the pipe. She could not help kissing him because she was in love with him.

"Tonight, my dear," Zoak told her, "you sleep in the bedroom and I will sleep in the living quarters on the couch."

"All right, thank you," Esapher said.

She was quite embarrassed because she had never been near a man before and she had wanted to kiss him. Little did she know that the little house that she found happiness and love in was destined to be her prison. The man Zoak was a wizard. He was sent to her by her Aunt Salo to keep her prisoner for three years.

The next day or so, Zoak told Esapher that he had to go away on a trip, but that he would see her again soon. She told him goodbye. She was sorry to see him go because she loved him so much. He locked the door when he left.

When Esapher got ready to go out and feed Sweep she found that she had been locked in. How she kicked and banged, but nothing she could do would bring anyone to her rescue because she was too far away from a neighbor. There was plenty of food for Esapher to eat but she was worried about Sweep. She did not know that Sweep was all right. He had plenty of food and water.

How she wished that Zoak would return. For two months Esapher stayed locked in her prison not being able to get out and get any fresh air.

Zoak the wizard had visited Salo and told her how Esapher was getting along.

"Is she still beautiful?" asked the witch.

"Yes," said the wizard. "With beauty and grace."

"Then you must destroy her beauty," the witch sneered. "She has disowned me. Go now, destroy her beauty. Maybe she will return to me."

The wizard bade the witch farewell and returned to the little house that had been destined to become Esapher's prison. She was fine but heartsick. The Wizard Zoak thought about how wonderful it would be to be a normal man and live a normal life with Esapher as his wife, to raise children. But being a wizard was another way of life, rather a lonely one.

He had become more than fond of Esapher, but he was a wizard and he had work to do. But to destroy her beauty, that he dreaded to do, for Esapher was the most beautiful woman that he had ever seen.

Salo the witch had cast a spell upon the wizard at birth. He remembered the tale. If a pretty woman would kill him three times, then he would again become a normal person. Then he would be out of Salo's power. He would never more have to do her bidding. He would not have to destroy Esapher's beauty, because he really loved her. The kiss that she had planted upon his lips stayed with him, and he could not forget her trusting innocence.

When he returned to the little house, he unlocked the door to Esapher's room. Esapher was sitting in the rocker, just staring.

"My dear," he asked her, "what's wrong?"

She was unable to answer him.

"I will have to use my powers," said the wizard. "The squab spell has taken effect. Esapher is in her prison in mind as well as in body."

Zoak went out and got a squab, picked three feathers and put them on running water.

"Carry Esapher's youth and beauty and mind from the three years of destruction. Let her not be a prisoner."

Zoak watched the three feathers being carried down the stream. When he returned to the house, Esapher was standing on the porch with her arms opened. He went into them.

"My darling Esapher," he told her. "I have a story to tell you about myself. I am…"

"Never mind," Esapher said. "I know that you are the wizard Zoak, and if I kill you three times then you will again be normal. Then you will marry me. I shall become your wife."

"How did you know, Esapher?"

"Before I went into my trance," Esapher told Zoak, "Sweep was at the window. I went to see if he was all right. As I looked at Sweep a change came over me. These things I found out in my trance."

"Then hurry and kill me, my dear."

Esapher cut off his head with a long knife. He immediately regained another. She watched it take form. She cut the second off, then the third. The fourth head formed more beautiful than the others and Zoak became the handsomest man ever. As Zoak changed, Sweep did too.

"I am not a horse," Sweep said. "I am Zoak's father. The witch, your aunt, cast a spell upon me when Zoak was born. I knew that someday my son would find out the truth."

They were all happy. Esapher fixed a hearty meal. They all sat down at the table happy as could be, and Sweep was the happiest of all because he was not eating hay and oats, but a really delicious meal cooked for him and his son by his daughter-in-law to be.